DOG'S
COLOURFUL DAY

VIKING

Published by the Penguin Group
Penguin Books Ltd, 80 Strand, London WC2R ORL, England
Penguin Putnam Inc., 375 Hudson Street, New York, New York 10014, USA
Penguin Books Australia Ltd, Ringwood, Victoria, Australia
Penguin Books Canada Ltd, 10 Alcorn Avenue, Toronto, Ontario, Canada M4V 3B2
Penguin Books India (P) Ltd, 11 Community Centre, Panchsheel Park, New Delhi – 110 017, India
Penguin Books (NZ) Ltd, Cnr Rosedale and Airborne Roads, Albany, Auckland, New Zealand
Penguin Books (South Africa) (Pty) Ltd, 24 Sturdee Avenue, Rosebank 2196, South Africa

Penguin Books Ltd, Registered Offices: 80 Strand, London WC2R ORL, England

www.penguin.com

First published in Canada by Prospero Books 2000

1 3 5 7 9 10 8 6 4 2

Copyright © Tucker Slingsby Ltd, 2000

Devised and produced by Tucker Slingsby Ltd, Berkeley House,
73 Upper Richmond Road, London SW15 2SZ
Design by Helen James
Typography by Richard Amari

Printed in Singapore

British Library Cataloguing in Publication Data
A CIP catalogue record for this book is available from the British Library

ISBN 0-670-91272-7

DOg's
COLOURFUL DAY

A Messy Story about Colours and Counting
Emma Dodd

VIKING

This is Dog.

As you can see,
Dog is white with
one black spot on
his left ear.

At breakfast time,
Dog sits under
the table, as usual.

Splat!

A drip of red jam
lands on his back.

Now Dog has
two spots.

After breakfast, Dog runs outside.

He slips past the man
painting the front door.

Splish!

His tail dips into
the blue paint.

Now Dog has three spots.

Dog runs to the park
and rolls on the grass.

Squash!

The grass makes a green
stain on his white coat.

Now Dog has four spots.

Dog follows a little boy
eating chocolate.

Squish!

The boy gives Dog a
chocolatey pat –
but no chocolate.

Now Dog has
five spots.

A bee buzzes up to
see what is going on.

Swish!

The bee drops yellow
pollen as it flies by.

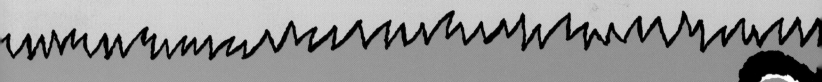

Now Dog has six spots.

Dog trots on
through the park.

Splosh!

A drop of pink
ice cream lands
on his right ear.

Now Dog has seven spots.

Time to go home.
Dog runs up the street.

Splash!

A bouncing ball splatters
Dog with grey mud.

Now Dog has eight spots.

In front of the gate,
Dog steps on a carton
of orange juice.

Splurt!

A patch of orange
appears on his leg.

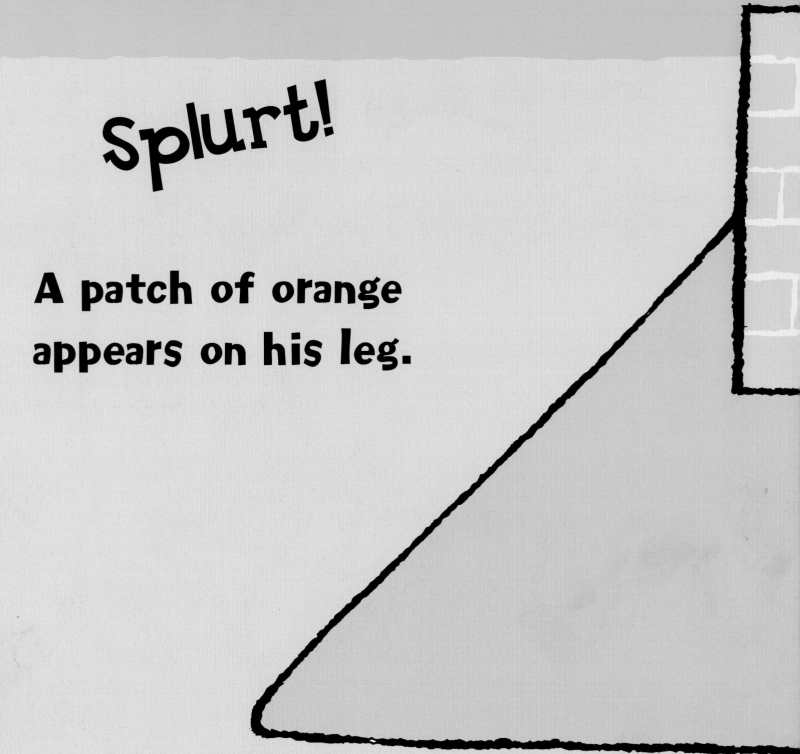

Now Dog has nine spots.

Dog races back inside the house and knocks right into Vicky.

"Silly Dog!"

Vicky's purple pen leaves a smudge on Dog's head.

Now Dog has
ten spots.

Vicky looks down at Dog.
She counts his colourful spots.

1   2   3   4   5

6   7   8   9   IO!

Vicky looks more closely.
Dog has . . .

a red spot of jam,

a blue blob of paint,

a green stain of grass,

a yellow patch of pollen,

a brown smear of chocolate,

a pink **drop** of ice cream,

a grey **splatter** of mud,

an orange **splash** of juice,

a purple **smudge** of ink,

and, of course, a black **spot** on his left ear!

"You need a bath, Dog!"

When Dog climbs into bed,
he has just one black spot
on his left ear.

Goodnight, Dog.

What a colourful day you've had!